Beautiful Me

Written by Sommer Gee

Illustration by Joseph Tilstra

Kaidipaw Publishing

© Kaidipaw Publishing, 2012
www.Kaidipaw.com
www.LessonswithLinus.com

ISBN: 978-1-939485-00-7

Printed in the USA
Signature Book Printing
www.sbpbooks.com

To my princess Maya!

In Memory of my Mom who was an amazing example of true beauty!

Find the paw print on each page!

There once was a little girl who was the most beautiful girl in the world. Her name was Princess Po.

Princess Po had many friends, but her best friend in the whole world was Sir Linus. One day Sir Linus asked Princess Po, "Do you know what makes you so beautiful?"

She thought for a minute and replied, "I think it's my hair. Everyone always says how pretty it is and how they would love to have hair like mine." Sir Linus replied, "Your hair is very pretty, but that is not what makes you beautiful."

"Well then it must be all of my gorgeous dresses. I have so many in different colors and styles," replied Princess Po. Sir Linus answered again, "Your dresses are amazing, but that is not what makes you beautiful."

"Then it must be all my cool toys," she said. "Everyone loves to play with them." "I love your toys too Princess Po, and they are fun to play with," he replied, "but that is not what makes you beautiful."

"Hmmm, I bet it's the way I dance. I practice very hard and take care of my body so that someday I can be the best dancer ever!" Princess Po said. "Your dancing gets better and better every day. I believe that you will be your best someday, but that is not what makes you beautiful either." Sir Linus replied.

Puzzled Princess Po thought and thought and sadly asked, "Sir Linus, if it's not my hair, my dresses, my toys or even my talent, then maybe I am not so beautiful after all."

"My dear Princess Po," Sir Linus began, "It's the thankfulness for your hair and the way you compliment others. It's the kindness you show when your friends borrow and wear your dresses. It's the patience you have while you wait your turn to use your toys. It's the excitement and happiness you have when you see someone else succeed."

"While you look pretty on the outside, it is the true joy and happiness in your heart that makes you beautiful. Never doubt how beautiful you are." Princess Po began to smile, "Thank you Sir Linus for showing me that when there is kindness and compassion in my heart it makes my whole self beautiful!"

1 Peter 3:3-4

"Braiding your hair doesn't make you beautiful. Wearing gold jewelry or fine clothes doesn't make you beautiful. Instead, your beauty comes from inside you. It is the beauty of a gentle and quiet spirit. Beauty like that doesn't fade away. God places great value on it."

YOU ARE BEAUTIFUL!